ROTHERHAM LIBRARY & INFORMATION SERVICE

D1494302

This book must be returned by the date specified at the time of issue as the DUE DATE FOR RETURN
The loan may be extended (personally, by post, telephone or online) for a further period, if the book is not required by another reader, by quoting the barcode / author / title.

Enquiries: 01709 336774

www.rotherham.gov.uk/libraries

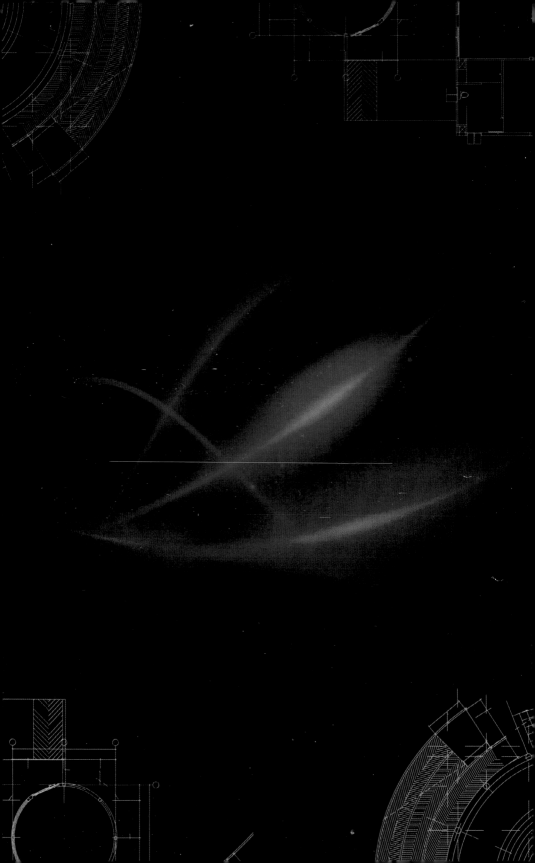

GALAXY
FOOTBALL CUP

Steve Barlow and Steve Skidmore

Illustrated by Santy Gutiérrez

EDGE
FRANKLIN WATTS

LONDON•SYDNEY

Franklin Watts
First published in Great Britain in 2019 by The Watts Publishing Group

Credits
Design Manager: Peter Scoulding
Cover Designer: Cathryn Gilbert
Illustrations: Santy Gutiérrez
HB ISBN 978 1 4451 5985 0
PB ISBN 978 1 4451 5986 7
Library ebook ISBN 978 1 4451 5987 4

Printed in China.

Franklin Watts
An imprint of
Hachette Children's Group
Part of The Watts Publishing Group
Carmelite House
50 Victoria Embankment
London EC4Y 0DZ

An Hachette UK Company
www.hachette.co.uk

www.franklinwatts.co.uk

THE BADDIES

Lord and
Lady Evil

Dr Y

They want to rule the galaxy.

THE GOODIES

Boo Hoo   Jet   Tip

They want to stop them.

7

8

"Wow!" said Tip. "I didn't know that I'd entered a competition! That is amazing!"

Jet shook her head. "No. That is suspicious."

Tip smiled. "Don't worry. Let's go! We're going to see the Hawks win!"

"I don't think so," said Jet. "This is too good to be true."

The final begins.

The horn blew for half-time.

"Let's get some drinks," said Jet.

"I'll have a large oil," said Boo Hoo.

They got their drinks and went back to their seats.

"Oh no," said Tip. "There are people blocking our view!"

"They weren't there before," said Jet.

"Ask them to move," said Tip. "Politely."

Dr Y laughed. "There was no competition. You fell for my trap! I am arresting you!"

"Oh yeah," said Jet. "You and whose army?"

Jet and Tip headed out of the exit.

"Oh no!" said Jet. "Look where we are!"

The Hawks' coach saw them. "We've got injured players. Get on the field now! There is only a minute left!"

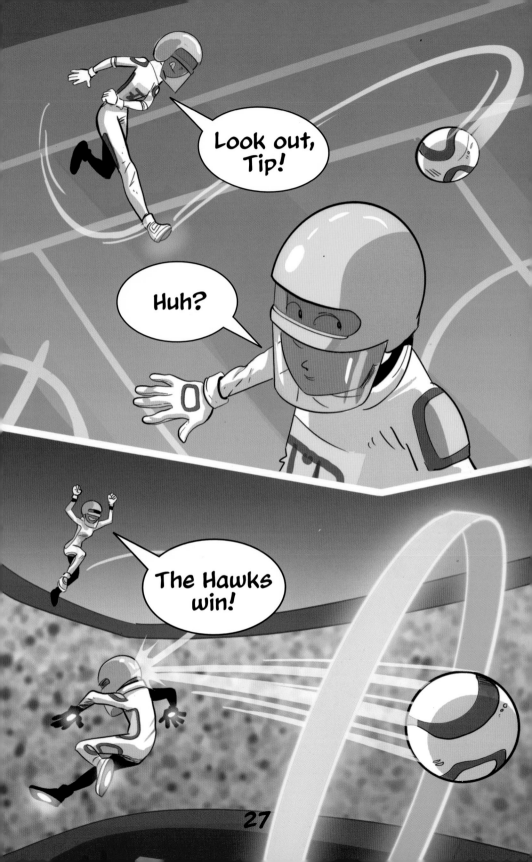

27

But then...